First American Edition 2014
Kane Miller, A Division of EDC Publishing

Text copyright © 2013 Sally Rippin
Illustrations copyright © 2013 Aki Fukuoka
Series design copyright © 2013 Hardie Grant Egmont

First published in Australia by Hardie Grant Egmont

For information contact:
Kane Miller, A Division of EDC Publishing
5402 S 122nd E Ave
Tulsa, OK 74146
www.kanemiller.com
www.myubam.com

Library of Congress Control Number: 2013953408

Printed and bound in the United States of America
12 13 14 15 16 17 18 19 20
ISBN: 978-1-61067-311-2

A Billie B. MYSTERY

Spooky House

By Sally Rippin

Illustrated by Aki Fukuoka

Kane Miller
A DIVISION OF EDC PUBLISHING

Chapter One

It's lunchtime and the weather is hot. Billie B. Brown and her friends sit under the pepper tree at the edge of the playground.

Billie pulls a banana sandwich out of her lunch box. Then she pulls out something wrapped in tissue paper.

"What's that?" Mika asks.

"Guess," says Billie, smiling secretively. She hands Mika the bundle of tissue paper. "Don't open it, though!"

Mika closes her eyes and feels through the tissue. "Hmmm. It has a long thin bit," she says slowly. "And a round bit. And it's hard."

"I know what it is," says Jack. He has already seen Billie's new present because he lives next door. Billie showed it to him yesterday.

"Don't tell!" says Billie.

"Can I see?" says Alex.

Mika hands him the package.

"Give us a clue?" asks Mika.

Billie grins. "It makes things bigger."

"A magnifying glass!" Mika says.

"You're right!" says Billie. She takes the package back from Alex and carefully unwraps it. There, glinting in the sunlight, is a brand-new magnifying glass. "My grandma gave it to me," she says proudly.

3

"Cool," Alex and Mika say together. They touch the glass with their fingertips.

"You can burn stuff with a magnifying glass," Alex says. "If we hold it over some dry leaves we could start a fire. I saw it on TV once."

"No way," says Jack. "That's dangerous! Mr. Benetto would be pretty angry if you burned the whole school down."

Billie beckons for her friends to listen closely and lowers her voice.

"Actually, I was thinking we could start a secret mystery club. We can use the magnifying glass to be spies and look for clues."

"It's detectives who use magnifying glasses, not spies," Alex says.

Billie rolls her eyes. Sometimes Alex acts like he knows **everything**. "That's what I meant," she says, shrugging. "Detectives."

"Aren't they the same thing?" Mika says.

"No," says Alex. "Detectives are like Sherlock Holmes. Spies are like James Bond."

"Can I be James Bond?" says Mika.

"I call Sherlock Holmes!" says Jack.

"That's not what I meant!" says Billie, feeling frustrated that her friends are being silly. "We'll be more like the Famous Five. Or the Secret Seven."

"But there's only four of us!" Jack grins. "Unless you want to invite Scraps?"

Alex woofs and Mika laughs.

Billie can't help grinning a little. But she wants her friends to listen. "Come on, I'm serious," she says.

"Where are we going to find a mystery around here, Billie?" Jack says. He swings his arms out wide.

"Unless you want to find out the mystery of the stinky lunch box?" Alex jokes.

"Or the missing pencil case?" Mika giggles.

Billie sighs. *Jack's right,* she thinks. *School isn't a very exciting place to explore. Neither are our homes. Even the park isn't very exciting anymore, now that we are big.*

Billie tries to think of a place where they might find a mystery to solve. She has to be **quick**. Already her friends have started talking about other things. If she doesn't think of something soon, they won't want to start a secret club with her at all!

Just then, Billie has an idea.
A super-duper idea! She knows
the perfect place. It's **mysterious**
and **spooky** and she is sure her
friends will be impressed. "I know
somewhere," she says loudly. "A really
scary place. But only super brave kids
would dare to go there."

"Where?" ask the others. They turn
to face her, suddenly interested
again.

Billie leans back against the
trunk of the tree and smiles.

She knows her friends are paying attention now. "The spooky house at the end of our street," she says.

Jack gasps. "The haunted house?"

Billie nods.

"There's no such thing as a haunted house," Alex scoffs. He crosses his arms against his chest.

Billie feels annoyed with Alex. Even though she is pretty sure there's no such thing as well, she still wants to make absolutely super sure.

11

Besides, she really wants to start a secret mystery club and Alex is ruining everything. So she ignores him and turns to Mika and Jack, putting on her spookiest voice.

"Sometimes when you walk past the house, you can hear **sawing** or **grinding** noises," she says. "That's the witch in there – grinding up bones!"

"Witches don't live in haunted houses," Alex laughs. "That's ghosts."

"There are ghosts, too," Billie adds. "They wait until a kid walks past on their own and then they catch them. Then the witch grinds up their bones and eats them!"

Jack and Mika **shiver**.

"No one has ever seen anyone go in," Billie says in her spooky voice. "Or come out." She is having fun making up the story.

Then she announces, "The first mystery of the Secret Mystery Club is to find out who is living in that old house at the end of our street.

Who is brave enough to come with me?" She holds up her magnifying glass to her eye.

Mika shoots up her hand. Alex puts up his hand, too, but he rolls his eyes like he still doesn't believe Billie's story.

Last of all, Jack puts up his hand, very slowly. He looks worried. Billie knows he is only putting up his hand because he doesn't want to be left behind.

Billie feels a teensy bit bad.

She didn't mean to scare Jack.
But she really, **really** wants to find
an exciting mystery for the Secret
Mystery Club to solve.

Jack will be okay, she thinks.

She hopes she is right.

Chapter Two

That weekend, Jack, Mika and Alex meet at Billie's house.

They all sit in a circle in Billie's room with the door tightly closed.

Billie has written a sign to put on the door.

It says:

Keep Out!
(Especially YOU, Noah!)
Secret meeting.
(No little kids allowed.)

Billie's little brother, Noah, can't read yet, but Billie hopes her parents will get the hint.

Billie doesn't mind playing with Noah some days, but not every day. And besides, Noah is much too young for secret mystery business.

Billie has borrowed the picnic basket from the kitchen cupboard. She hands it around the group. One by one her friends put in a bag of candy each. They have bought them with their own money.

Billie drops her candy in last, then reads out their plan from her special secret notebook, which has a real lock and key. She has written in her tiniest extra small handwriting so that she can use her magnifying glass to read it.

She **squints** down at the paper. "The Secret Mystery Club's first mystery. What is going on in the Haunted House? Is there really a witch living there?" she reads. "Plan: Two people knock on the door and pretend that they are selling candy for school.

The other two will look through a window or over the back fence. Look for any clues and report back to the SMC as soon as possible."

"What's the SMC?" Mika asks.

"Code for Secret Mystery Club," Billie says. "Whatever happens, nobody must know about our club. OK?"

"OK," agree the other three.

"Maybe we should have a secret call?" Alex suggests.

"Good idea," says Billie. She is happy that Alex seems to be enjoying the mystery now. "How about a whistle? Like this." She puts her fingers to her mouth and whistles loudly.

Next door, Jack's dog Scraps starts barking. Billie giggles.

"Too obvious," says Alex.

"And I can't whistle," admits Mika.

"How about a bird call?" says Jack.

All of them begin **squawking** and **whistling** and making all kinds of bird noises. *Too-whit-to-whoo! Caw! Caw! Cheep, cheep!*

Finally, Alex does a rooster crow and everyone bursts out laughing.

"All right, a rooster crow it is!" Billie giggles. "Now, this is the important decision. Who is going around the front of the spooky house and who's going around the back?"

Everyone looks at each other.

"I don't really want to knock on the front door," Jack says.

"Well, you're a good climber," Billie says. "So maybe you and Alex should look over the back fence?"

Alex shrugs. "OK with me. Jack?"

Jack shrugs. "I guess so." He chews a fingernail nervously.

Billie grins. "Will you come with me then, Mika?" she asks. "We'll knock on the front door."

Mika nods **bravely**.

"If a witch comes to the front door, we'll just run away," Billie explains.

"What about us?" Jack yelps.

"You run, too," Billie says. "If we get separated, meet back here, OK?"

The others nod.

Billie sticks out her hand, palm facing downward. "Put your hand on mine," she says.

Everyone puts their palms face down on Billie's. Then she bounces their hands up and down and crows loudly like a rooster. The others join in.

"Cock-a-doodle-dooo!"

Billie looks at Jack out of the corner of her eye.

She can see that he is trying his best to crow like a rooster.

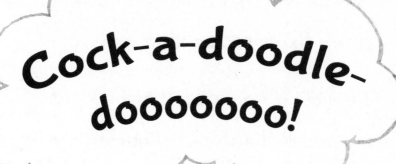

But he is so nervous that he sounds more like a **squawking** hen!

I wonder if I should tell him it's just a game, Billie thinks. *But then the others would think I was tricking them. And the Secret Mystery Club would have no mystery to solve!*

Chapter Three

Billie makes her way down the street with the rest of the Secret Mystery Club.

When they get close to the spooky house, they split into two groups. Alex and Jack slip around the side of the house.

Billie and Mika wait a minute, then they walk up to the front gate. This is the closest Billie has ever been to the spooky house. Usually when she and Jack walk past, they cross to the other side of the street.

She feels a **buzzy** mix of excitement and fear. Even though she knows that a witch probably doesn't live there, her heart is still beating very fast.

Billie slowly pushes open the front gate. It lets out a long squeal.

A black cat scoots across the front porch and around the side of the house.

"A witch's cat!" Billie whispers to Mika. "That is definitely a witch's cat."

Mika's eyes become as round as moons. "Are you sure we should knock on the door?" she says.

"Of course!" says Billie, but she feels her heart beat even faster.

The front yard is a tangled mess of weeds and bushes.

Billie and Mika tiptoe along the cracked path toward the pale green door. The tall gray house is faded and peeling. Big flakes of paint curl up to show the silvery boards beneath.

"This is *so* a witch's house!" Billie hisses.

"Stop it, Billie!" Mika says. She stops walking and screws up her face. "Or I'm going home!"

Billie giggles. *Even Mika believes my spooky stories now!* she thinks.

"There's no such thing as ghosts and witches, Mika!" she says. "Everyone knows that."

Mika frowns. "That's not what you said before."

"I know, but I was just fooling around," Billie says. "I wanted to have a mystery to solve! We'll just knock on the door to see if anyone lives here, and then we can go home." She grabs Mika's hand.

They step up to the door. Billie lifts a hand, pauses for a second, then gives the door three loud knocks.

The street is completely quiet except for the **rustle** of wind in the trees. In the distance, a car starts up.

"There's no one here!" Mika says after a moment. She looks relieved. "Come on, let's find the others."

"Wait!" says Billie. "I think I hear something." She puts her ear to the door.

From deep inside the house comes the strange noise she has heard before. A whirring machine noise, grinding and crushing.

"That must be the witch's kid-crushing machine!" Billie says in a low voice to Mika.

Mika turns as pale as a ghost. "Billie!" she says angrily. "You just said there's no such thing as witches. Now you're *trying* to scare me! I'm going back to your house. This isn't fun anymore!" She marches back down the path.

"Wait!" whispers Billie. "I think I *can* hear someone. Really!"

But Mika stomps through the gate and closes it behind her. Then she jogs around the side of the house to look for Alex and Jack.

Billie watches Mika go. She feels a bit bad for scaring her friends.

This house is pretty **spooky**. Maybe this wasn't the best place to look for a mystery after all.

Billie listens to the noises from deep inside the house. Whirring, grinding, creaking noises.

Then a noise like footsteps.
Slow, heavy footsteps on creaking
floorboards. Coming closer.
And closer.

Suddenly, the door is flung open.
Billie looks up. And gasps.

Standing in front of her is the
scariest woman Billie has ever
seen. She has long white hair and
is wearing a long black dress. Just
like a real witch! When Billie looks
at her long skinny fingers, she sees
that they are spattered with red.

"Hello?" the woman says. Her voice is croaky like a frog. She curls back her lips to show a line of yellow teeth.

Billie drops her basket of candy in fright. She runs down the path and through the rickety gate, her heart pounding in her ears. Then she runs all the way home.

Chapter Four

"She is definitely a witch!" Billie tells the others as soon as they are all safely back in Billie's bedroom. "I saw her and I'm telling you, she's definitely a witch!"

Mika narrows her eyes. "There's no such thing as witches," she says.

Then she turns to the others. "Billie was just making up stories all along. She told me so."

Alex frowns. "I knew it!" he says in a know-it-all voice.

"But there was a witch! A real one. I promise!" Billie says. "She had long white hair and a long black dress. And she had a black cat. You saw the cat, Mika!"

Mika crosses her arms. "There wasn't anyone in that house, Billie. You're just trying to scare us."

"Yeah," Alex says. "Jack looked over the fence. The backyard is all overgrown. It's just an empty house, Billie."

"But she came just after you left!" Billie insists. "She was really **creepy**. And she had red stuff on her hands. I'm not saying it was blood, but…"

"Stop it, Billie!" Mika says. "I'm not playing with you if you keep trying to scare us."

"Me neither," Alex says. "This isn't fun anymore. I'm going home."

"Me too!" says Mika.

Billie looks at her three friends in **shock**. "But what about the club?" she says in a little voice. "Our Secret Mystery Club?"

Billie looks at Jack hopefully. His cheeks turn pink and he looks away.

"I'll only play if you stop scaring us," he mumbles. "Nobody likes your scary stories, Billie."

"But…" Billie says, then she stops herself. It's no use. They will never believe her now.

If only I hadn't played tricks on them!
she thinks. *Then they'd believe me.*

"OK," she says, hanging her head.
"I won't talk about witches
anymore. I promise."

"Cross your heart?" Mika says.

Billie nods. "And hope to die."

Chapter Five

The next day, Billie can't stop thinking about the spooky woman. *What if she really is a witch?* she thinks. *What if she comes looking for me?* A shiver passes through her.

She goes downstairs to sit in the kitchen with her family.

Being with her family always makes her feel better.

Noah is sitting at his little table, scribbling on paper with crayons.

"Hey, Noah," Billie says. She pats him on his soft brown hair. He smiles and hands her his drawing.

"Oh, that's nice!" says Billie. She looks down at the red and yellow scribbles across the page. "What is it?"

"Giwaffe!" says Noah proudly.

"Oh yes, of course!" says Billie, grinning. She turns the paper around three times, but she can still only see scribble, no giraffe.

"Hey, Billie, have you seen the picnic basket?" her dad says. He is on a stepladder searching in the top cupboards.

"Oh!" says Billie. She suddenly remembers. "Um, why?"

"Well, we thought we'd go for a picnic this afternoon because it's such a nice day," Billie's mom says.

"But we can't find the picnic basket anywhere. You haven't been playing with it, have you, Billie?"

Billie feels her cheeks get hot and her ears sting. "Um, no!" she says in a squeaky voice.

"Billie?" says her mom, looking at her suspiciously.

"Oh, that's right. I borrowed it," she says. "For a game I was playing."

"Oh, good," Billie's dad says, climbing down the stepladder. "I've been looking for it everywhere!

Can you run and get it?"

In her mind Billie sees the basket sitting on the front step of the spooky house. "Um, well, I don't have it anymore," she says. "I, er, I lent it to someone."

"Who?" says her dad.

"Jack," Billie says. He is the first person she can think of.

"Well, can you go and get it?" Billie's mom says. She sounds a little bit **annoyed**.

Billie slips down off her stool and trudges toward the back door. "OK," she says, worried. "I'll go and get it now. I'll be back soon."

Billie slides open the back door and runs down the steps toward the hole in the fence. Then she **squeezes** through the gap and into Jack's backyard. Now that Billie is getting bigger it's harder to slip through, but it is still the quickest way to visit her best friend.

"Is Jack home?" Billie asks Jack's dad when he opens the back door.

"Sure, Billie," he says. "He's upstairs. Shall I call him down?"

"No, that's OK. I'll go up," says Billie. She runs up the stairs two at a time and swings open his bedroom door. Jack is sitting on the floor building a Lego spaceship.

"Jack!" she says, panting. "I need your help! I'm in **big** trouble."

Chapter Six

Billie explains what's happened and Jack listens carefully.

"So I need you to come with me to get the basket back," she says. "I'm too scared to go on my own."

"All right," Jack says, packing away

his Lego. "But no talking about witches or ghosts or anything else spooky like that, OK?"

"OK," Billie promises. "Thanks, Jack. You're the best."

Jack and Billie hurry downstairs. "Billie and I are just taking Scraps for a walk," Jack calls out to his parents.

"OK," his mom calls back. "But only for half an hour. We're going to your grandma's for lunch."

Scraps jumps up and down excitedly when he sees the leash.

Billie and Jack walk him out the front door and along the sidewalk, toward the spooky house. Outside, lots of people are walking their dogs. Billie and Jack wave at Mr. Ahmed from across the street with his tiny poodle. Scraps and Mr. Ahmed's poodle bark at each other.

As they get closer to the spooky house, Billie feels her heart begin to jump around. *What if the witch sees us coming?* she worries.

What if she catches us and eats us for dinner?

Soon they arrive. Billie looks up at the cracked window on the top floor glinting in the sunlight. It blinks back at her and she shivers.

Jack ties Scraps to the fence and he and Billie open the gate as quietly as they can. **Screeeee!**, it squeals. Billie freezes, looking up at the front door.

"Oh no!" she says. "The basket's gone! The wi— I mean, the woman must have taken it!"

"Well, I guess someone lives here after all," Jack says calmly. "Come on. We'll just knock on the door and ask for the basket back." He grabs Billie's hand and pulls her to the door.

"No!" says Billie, pulling away. She stands shaking beside Scraps at the gate. "Don't worry about the basket, Jack. Let's go home! I'll just tell Mom and Dad I lost it!"

"Billie," says Jack, shaking his head and looking a little annoyed.

"There's no such thing as witches, remember? You made that story up."

"I know!" Billie says. "It's just that…" But before she can finish, Jack has begun rapping on the front door. Almost immediately, it swings open and the tall white-haired lady is there. She looks even scarier than she did the day before.

"Hello again!" she says to Billie. "You've come back, have you?" She smiles her yellow-toothed smile.

"Um, we left a basket on your doorstep," Jack explains. "We were just wondering if we could have it back? Billie's parents need it for a picnic."

"Oh yes," says the woman, resting her hand on Jack's shoulder.

Billie sees the **horrible** red splashes on her fingers.

"I took it inside," the witchy woman continues. "Why don't you come in? I've just got something in the oven that I need to check on."

Billie feels all her blood drain down to her feet. *Children,* she thinks. *I bet that's what she has in her oven!* She turns to run away, but then, to her surprise, Jack answers the scary old lady.

"Sure!" he says, without looking at Billie. Then he steps right into the woman's dark hallway.

"Jack!" Billie calls out. Her voice comes out like a terrified **squawk**.

Jack turns and smiles curiously. "Can you watch Scraps for me?" he says. "I'll be back in a minute."

Billie's mouth drops open in disbelief. *Jack is going inside?* she thinks. *But he is the scarediest person, I know! Maybe the witch has cast a spell over him?*

But before she can say or do anything, the woman closes her front door.

With Jack on the other side.

Chapter Seven

"Jack! Jack!" Billie calls out quietly. She doesn't want the witch to come out and catch her too! But it is no use. The door stays firmly closed.

I have to do something! Billie thinks. *This is all my fault!*

Just then, she remembers.

The house has a side window!

She sprints around the corner to

see if she can spot Jack inside.

Billie finds the window, but it is too

high for her to see through.

Quickly, she looks around for
something to climb. On the
path by the fence is an old
wooden plank.

Billie leans it up against the side
of the house and wedges the end
under the windowsill.

Then carefully, **carefully**, she inches her way up. The plank wibbles and wobbles, but Billie holds on tight. Soon her eyes are in line with the windowsill.

Billie peers through the dusty glass into the dark room. What she sees nearly makes her fall off the plank in fright.

Ghosts! Billie sees ghosts! Big tall eerie ghosts. Wide shadowy spooky ghosts. Pale white shapes in the big gloomy room.

Billie jumps off the plank, her
heart beating like a drum. It's not
just a witch that lives in there,
but ghosts too!

Should I go back home and get help?
Billie wonders. *But what if I'm too
late? What if the witch has already put
Jack into her bone-crushing machine?
Or in the oven!*

Just then, she hears voices coming
from the backyard. A loud cackle
and then — Jack's voice! He's still
alive! Billie feels dizzy with relief.
She runs up to the side fence.

She doesn't want to climb it in case the witch spots her. So she searches desperately for a hole to peek through. Luckily, a piece of the rickety old fence breaks off in her hand. Billie peers through the crack.

Through the hole she sees an overgrown backyard full of tall grass and gnarly old trees. All around the backyard are strange metal objects of all different shapes and sizes. Some of them are like weird machines. Others look like strange clockwork creatures.

Billie hears the voices again.
She pulls away some more of the
wooden fence to see better.
When she pushes her face to the
hole, the splintery wood prickles
her cheek.

"Jack!" she whispers. "Jack!"

She even does their secret rooster
call quietly, but he still doesn't
reply.

Then, when she is about to lose all
hope, she sees him.

"Jack?" Billie can't believe her eyes.

Chapter Eight

There in the backyard is Jack and the witch. They are walking around looking at all the weird mechanical creatures. The woman is carrying the basket.

As Billie watches, Jack puts his hand into it and pulls out a piece of candy. Billie blinks and looks again. But there is nothing wrong with her eyes. Jack is really walking around the backyard with the strange witchy lady – eating candy!

At that moment, Jack turns around. He sees Billie's face pressed against the hole in the fence.

"Billie?" he calls. "What are you doing there?" He jogs toward the side gate to let Billie in.

Billie stands at the gate, her eyes wide and her mouth open.

"What…?" she stammers.

Jack grins. "You weren't worried about me, were you?" he whispers.

The woman in black **swoops** over. "Sorry to keep you waiting, love," she says. "I was just showing Jack some of my sculptures."

She swings her arms wide, pointing at the strange metal objects all around the backyard. "Oh, and excuse me for eating your candy. I just couldn't resist it! But I'll give Jack's mom some money for more when I see her next."

The woman puts out her hand for Billie to shake. When Billie stands frozen, she looks down at her red splotchy fingers. "Oh, the paint's dry, love. It just won't wash off! I've been painting my new sculptures red."

"More sculptures?" asks Jack. "Cool. You have so many!"

"Yes! They're inside, if you want to see them? I've covered them with sheets for now so they don't get dusty. Grinding metal and sawing wood creates such a lot of mess!"

Billie blinks. All the words she has in her head get stuck in her mouth.

"I think we'd better get going, actually," Jack says. "Billie's mom is waiting for her basket. Maybe we can drop in and see the rest of your sculptures another day, Mrs. Wellington?"

"Oh, please. Call me Andrea," she says. "Mrs. Wellington makes me feel so old! All right then, kids. Do drop in any time. And thanks for the candy!"

Jack waves good-bye to Andrea at her gate. Her yellow teeth gleam in the sunlight as she waves back.

Chapter Nine

"*Andrea?*" says Billie to Jack, when they have rounded the corner.

Jack grins a little sheepishly and shrugs. "I talked to Mom yesterday. I know you said we weren't to talk to anyone about the Secret Mystery Club, but you scared us so much."

"But why didn't you tell me she was friends with your mom on the way here?" Billie says crossly. "I was scared, Jack! Really scared!"

Jack bends down to scratch Scraps behind his ears. Then he looks up and gives her a strange look. "It's not a nice feeling, is it?" he says seriously. "When a friend tries to scare you on purpose."

Billie feels her cheeks get hot. She looks down at the ground.

Jack is right, she thinks. *It was mean of me to scare him. And Mika and Alex. It serves me right that Jack wanted to scare me back.*

"Sorry," she says quietly. "I wanted to have a mystery to solve so much. And I thought it was just a bit of fun. But I guess I got carried away."

Jack smiles and passes Billie the basket. "That's OK. Come on, we'd better get back. We don't want to scare our parents now, do we?"

Billie laughs. She walks alongside Jack swinging the empty basket.

She feels **buzzy** with relief.

"But come on," she says, shaking her head. "You have to admit, it really does look like a witch's house! And, well, she does kind of dress like a witch."

"I know!" says Jack. "You should have seen how messy her house was inside. I guess she's too busy making her sculptures to clean up. Mom says she's a famous artist. Her sculptures were pretty cool.

You should come see them with me one day."

"Maybe," says Billie. She thinks about the strange white shapes she saw when she was peeking through the side window, and tries to imagine what weird sculptures might be hidden under there. "She still spooks me a little though."

Jack laughs. "You? But you're the bravest person I know, Billie! You're not scared of anyone!"

Billie grins. Then she puts on a spooky old witch voice. "Obviously not as brave as you, my friend!"

Scraps **barks** and the two of them jog along the street. They arrive at Billie's house and Jack waits for her to go inside.

Just then, Billie sees something white on the doorstep. "Jack! Come here!" she calls.

Jack bounds up to Billie with Scraps close behind. "What is it?" he says.

Billie bends down to pick up the
thing at her feet. It is an envelope,
made from stiff white paper.

They peer down at the curly black
writing on the front and read:

For the Secret Mystery Club
Urgent!

Billie gasps. She tears open the
envelope and pulls out a large piece
of folded white paper.

"What does it say?" Jack asks, trying to peer over her shoulder.

"I don't know," Billie says slowly. She turns the paper around and around. "I think it's in code."

He and Billie stare at the paper. It has strange black squiggles running across it.

"Wow," says Jack.

"I'll bring it to school on Monday," Billie says excitedly. "It looks like the Secret Mystery Club has our first real mystery to uncover!"

To be continued...

A HIGHER JUSTICE